ISBN 0 86112 983 0
Published by Brimax Books Ltd, Newmarket, England 1994.
Printed in Spain.

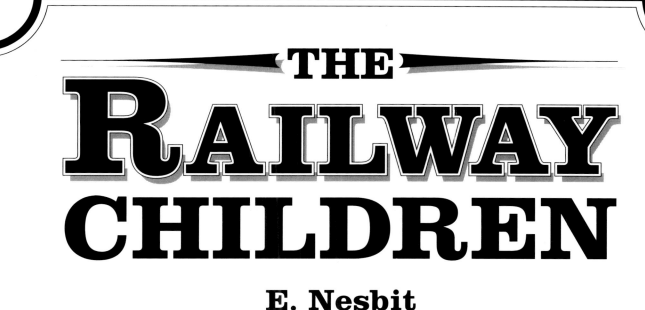

THE RAILWAY CHILDREN

E. Nesbit

Adapted by **John Escott**

Illustrated by **Mark Viney**

BRIMAX ◆ NEWMARKET ◆ ENGLAND

Introduction

One evening, the lives of Bobby, Peter and Phyllis change forever when their father is mysteriously called away. Before they know it, they and their mother have left their home in London and are living in the country. Close to their new home is the railway station and soon, Bobby, Peter and Phyllis are The Railway Children. They wave to trains, befriend the Station Master and Porter and even save a train and passengers from certain disaster. But it is their friendship with a certain old gentleman who travels by train every day that proves to be the most important feature of their new lives.

Contents

The Beginning of Things

They were not railway children to begin with. They were just ordinary children who lived in London, in an ordinary red-brick house, with their Father and Mother. There were three of them. Roberta, who was always called Bobbie, was the eldest. Of course, Mothers never have favourites, but if their mother *had* had a favourite, it would have been Bobbie. Next came Peter, who wanted to be an engineer when he grew up; and the youngest was Phyllis.

Mother was always ready to play with the children, and to help them with their home-lessons. And she wrote stories to read to them after tea. These three lucky children always had everything they needed: pretty clothes, good fires, heaps of toys. You will think they ought to have been very happy. And so they were, but they did not know *how* happy until the pretty life in London was over, and they had to live a very different life indeed.

The dreadful change came quite suddenly.

Peter had his tenth birthday, and among his presents was a model engine which soon became his favourite. But exactly three days after he had been given it, the engine suddenly went off with a bang!

Peter was very upset. The others said he cried, but Peter said his eyes were red because he had a cold. Father had been away in the country for three or four days, but when he returned Peter told him about the engine.

Father looked at it carefully. 'Hm,' he said.

'Is there no hope?' said Peter, in an unsteady voice.

'Hope? Yes, of course,' said Father, cheerfully. 'We'll mend it on Saturday afternoon.'

Just then, there was a knock at the front door.

'Now who can that be?' said Father.

Ruth, the parlour-maid, came in and said that two gentlemen wanted to see the master. 'I've shown them into the library, Sir,' she said.

'Get rid of them quickly, dear,' said Mother. 'It's nearly the children's bedtime.'

But Father did not seem to be able to get rid of the gentlemen quickly. Mother tried to pass the time by telling the children a story, but they could hear the voices in the other room. Father's voice sounded louder and different.

Ruth came back into the room. 'Please'm,' she said, 'the master wants you to step into the library. I think he's had bad news. Better be ready for the worst.'

Mother went into the library and there was more talking. Then the children heard a cab arrive, and the sound of boots going down the steps. Then the cab drove away and the front door was shut.

Mother came in, white-faced, her eyes big and shining.

'It's bedtime,' she said. 'Ruth will put you to bed.'

'But you promised we could stay up late because Father's home,' said Phyllis.

'Father's been called away — on business,' said Mother. 'Go to bed, darlings.'

Bobbie lingered after the others had gone. 'It wasn't bad news was it, Mammy? Is anyone dead or —'

'Nobody's dead,' said Mother. 'I can't tell you anything tonight, my pet. Please, go now.'

When they came down to breakfast the next morning, Mother had already gone out. It was nearly seven o'clock before she came home, looking so ill and tired that the children did not like to ask her questions. She sank into an armchair and had a cup of tea.

'Now, my darlings,' she said eventually. 'Those men last night did bring some bad news. Father will be away some time. I am very worried about it, and I want you all to help by being good and not quarrelling.'

'Is it something to do with the Government?' asked Bobbie. For Father worked in a Government office.

'Yes,' said Mother. 'But don't worry, my darlings, it will all come right in the end.'

After that, Mother was nearly always out. And the servants seemed to know more than they told about the bad news that the gentlemen had brought to Father. Then Peter was very naughty one day, and Ruth the parlour-maid said, 'If you don't mend your ways you'll go where your precious Father's gone!'

When Bobbie told her Mother this the next day, Ruth was sent away.

Then came the time when Mother went to bed and stayed there for two days, and the Doctor came and the children had to creep about the house. It seemed as if the world was coming to an end.

Mother came down to breakfast one morning, looking very pale. She smiled as well as she could, and said, 'Now, my pets, everything is settled. We're going to leave this house and go and live in the country. Such a dear little white house, I know you'll love it.'

A whirling week of packing followed – chairs, tables, crockery, blankets, carpets, candlesticks and saucepans, as well as all their clothes. Then, late one afternoon, a cab came and took them to the station and they got on a train.

At first, they enjoyed looking out of the train window, but when it grew dark, the children became sleepier and sleepier. No one knew how

long they had been asleep when Mother shook them gently and said, 'Wake up, dears. We're here.'

They stood shivering on the draughty platform whilst their baggage was unloaded. Then they watched the engine puff and blow itself away, and the tail-lights of the guard's van disappear into the darkness.

'We have to walk,' said Mother. 'There are no cabs here.'

A man with a cart took their baggage, and the walk was dark and muddy. There were no gas-lamps on the road, and Phyllis fell into a puddle. The road went uphill, then a long gate was opened and they went across fields. Presently, a shape appeared in the darkness.

'That's the house,' said Mother. 'I wonder why Mrs Viney has shut the shutters.'

'Who's Mrs Viney?' asked Bobbie.

'The woman I paid to clean the place and get our supper,' said Mother.

'Your train was late,' said the cart man. 'She'll have gone home.'

'But she's got the key,' said Mother.

'She'll have left it under the doorstep,' he said. He took the lantern off his cart and stooped to look. 'Aye, here it is.'

He unlocked the door and went in, putting his lantern down. There was a candle on the table and he lit it. The thin little light showed a kitchen with a stone floor but with no fire, just dead ashes. Then there was a scampering, rustling sound that seemed to come from inside the walls.

'It's only rats,' the cart man told them.

And he went out and shut the door. The sudden draught blew out the candle.

'Oh, dear,' said Phyllis. 'I wish we hadn't come!'

Peter's Coal Mine

'Well, you've often wanted something to happen,' said Mother, 'and now it has. This is quite an adventure, isn't it? I told Mrs Viney to have our supper ready. I suppose she's laid it in the dining room. Let's go and see.'

The dining room had dark wood from floor to ceiling, and a muddled maze of dusty furniture from their old home. There was a table and there were chairs, but there was no supper.

'What a horrid old woman!' said Mother. 'She's walked off with the money and not got us anything to eat.'

'Shan't we have any supper?' said a dismayed Phyllis.

"Oh, yes, we can unpack one of the big cases,' said Mother. 'I brought food from the old house.'

The girls lit some candles, then Bobbie made a fire whilst Mother laid out the food. Everyone was very, very tired, but they cheered up at the sight of the rather odd supper – biscuits, sardines, preserved ginger, cooking raisins, candied peel and marmalade – with ginger wine and water to drink.

After supper, they made the beds.

'Good night, chickies,' said Mother.

And the house was soon silent.

Next morning, Bobbie woke Phyllis by gently pulling her hair.

'Wake up!' said Bobbie. 'We're in the new house – don't you remember? I've woken Peter. He'll be dressed as soon as we are.'

They lit the fire, put the kettle on and arranged the crockery for breakfast. Then they went outside into the bright, fresh morning.

The house stood in a field, and the thatched roof of the kitchen sloped down low. On it were stone-crop and wallflowers, and even a clump of purple flag flowers.

'This is prettier then our old house,' said Phyllis. 'I wonder what the garden's like.'

But somehow they couldn't find the garden. There was a yard at the back of the house, and across it were stables and outbuildings. It was hilly country, and down below they could see the railway line, and the black yawning mouth of a tunnel. The station was out of sight, but there was a bridge with tall arches running across one end of the valley.

'Never mind the garden,' said Peter. 'Let's go down and look at the railway. There might be trains passing.'

'We can see them from here,' said Bobbie. 'Let's sit down.'

So they all sat on a flat grey stone in the grass in the warm sun. And when Mother came out to look for them at eight o'clock, she found them fast asleep and had to wake them.

'I've discovered another room,' she told them.

The room opened out of the kitchen. In the half-darkness of the night before they had mistaken it for a cupboard. But it was a little square room, and there was a table set for supper. There was cold roast beef, bread and butter, cheese, and a pie.

'There's a note from Mrs Viney,' said Mother. 'Her son-in-law has broken his arm, and she had to get home early. She's coming this morning at ten.'

Their supper made a lovely, if unusual, breakfast. The children thought it was funny having apple pie for breakfast.

For the rest of the day, they helped Mother unpack and arrange things, and it was quite late in the afternoon when she said, 'There, that'll do for today. I'll lie down for an hour before supper.'

The three children looked at each other and, without saying a word, knew where they were going. To the railway!

As soon as they set off, they saw where the garden had hidden itself. It was behind the stables and had a high wall around it.

'Never mind the garden now,' said Peter. 'Let's get to the railway.'

It was a downhill journey, over smooth short turf, ending in a wooden fence. And there was the railway with its shining metal lines; the telegraph wires and posts, and the signals. They climbed on to the fence, and suddenly there was a rumbling sound coming from the dark mouth of the tunnel. Next moment, a train rushed out with a shriek and a snort and slid noisily past them, the pebbles on the line jumping and rattling under it.

'It was like a great dragon tearing by!' said Bobbie, afterwards. 'Did you feel it fan us with its hot wings?'

'I never thought we should get so near to a train as this,' said Peter, his face full of excitement.

'I wonder if that train was going to London,' said Bobbie. 'London is where Father is.'

'Let's go down to the station and find out,' said Peter.

They walked along the edge of the line, the telegraph wires humming over their heads. Never before had they passed so close to a signal box, or walked on the very sleepers that the rails lay on. At last they reached the station and climbed up the sloping end of the platform.

There were a great many lines crossing at the station, but some just ran into a yard and stopped. Here there were trucks standing on rails, and a big heap of coal with a white line near the top of the coal-black

wall. When the Porter came out of his room, Peter asked him about the white line.

'It's to mark how much coal there is, so we'll know if anyone steals it. So don't you go off with any in your pockets, young gentleman!' said the Porter, with a smile.

Time went by and they soon got used to being without Father, though they did not forget him. And they got used to not going to school, and to seeing very little of Mother. She stayed in her upstairs room, writing, and came down at tea-time and read aloud the stories she had written.

More than once, Mother told them they were 'quite poor now', but there was always enough to eat and they wore the same nice clothes they had always worn. But in June came three wet days when it was very cold, and everybody shivered.

'Can we light a fire?' Bobbie asked.

'No, my darling,' said Mother. 'We mustn't have fires in June, coal is so expensive.'

After tea, Peter said to his sisters, 'I have an idea.'

'What's that?' they asked.

'I shan't tell you,' he said, 'because it may be wrong and I don't want to drag you into it. If Mother asks where I am, say I'm playing at mines.'

'What sort of mines?' asked Bobbie.

'Coal mines,' answered Peter, and would say no more.

Two nights later, Peter told the girls to follow him and to bring the Roman Chariot. The Roman Chariot was an old pram, and Bobbie and Phyllis pushed it after Peter as he led the way down towards the station.

Peter stopped by some rocks in the grass, and between them was a small heap of coal. 'Here's the first coal from St Peter's Mine,' he said. 'We'll take it home in the chariot.'

Three journeys were made, taking the coal and adding it to the heap in the cellar. Afterwards, Peter went out alone and came back very black.

'I've been to my coal mine,' he said, mysteriously. 'Tomorrow evening, we'll bring some more coal back in the chariot.'

But then came the dreadful night when the Station Master waited by the coal heap in the station yard until he saw a small dark shape scrabbling amongst the coal. He moved forward and grabbed a collar.

'I've caught you at last, you young thief!' he said.

And there was Peter, held firmly by his jacket.

'I – I'm not a thief,' Peter said, as steadily as he could. 'I'm a coal miner.'

'You're coming to the station with me,' the Station Master told him.

'Oh no!' came a cry from the darkness.

'Not the police station!' said another voice.

'Not yet,' said the Station Master. 'The Railway Station first. But how

many of you are there?'

'Only us,' said Bobbie and Phyllis, coming out of the shadows of the yard.

'It's our fault, as much as Peter's,' said Bobbie. 'We helped him carry away the coal, and we knew where he got it.'

'No, you didn't,' said Peter.

'Yes we did,' said Bobbie. 'We knew all the time. We only pretended we didn't.'

The Station Master looked at them closely. 'Why, you're the children from Three Chimneys house. So nicely dressed, too. Don't you know it's wicked to steal?'

'I didn't think it was stealing,' said Peter. 'I thought if I took it from the middle of the heap, it would be like mining. And it will take you thousands of years to burn up all that coal and get to the middle.'

'But why did you do it?' said the Station Master.

'Mother says we're too poor to have a fire,' Peter replied. 'We always had fires at our other house, and –'

'Don't!' whispered Bobbie.

The Station Master rubbed his chin, thoughtfully. 'Well,' he said. 'I'll overlook it this once. But remember, young gentleman, stealing is stealing, whether you call it mining or not.'

And the children knew he was speaking the truth.

'Now,' said the Station Master, 'run along home.'

The Old Gentleman

 fter this, the children decided to keep away from the station – but they could not keep away from the railway. They soon began to know the hours when certain trains passed, and even gave them names. The 9.15 up was called the Green Dragon. The 10.7 down was the Worm of Wantley. And the midnight express, whose shriek sometimes woke them from their dreams, was named the Fearsome Fly-by-Night.

The old gentleman travelled on the Green Dragon. He was a very nice-looking old gentleman, with white hair and a top hat, but the first thing they noticed about him was his hand.

'The Green Dragon is going where Father is,' said Phyllis, one morning when they were sitting on the fence. 'Let's all wave as it goes by. If it's a magic dragon, it will understand and take our love to Father.'

So when the Green Dragon came shrieking out of the tunnel, the three children stood on the fence and waved their handkerchiefs – and out of a first-class carriage, a hand waved back! It was the old gentleman's hand, and it held a newspaper.

After this, it became quite usual to exchange waves. The children liked to think that the old gentleman knew Father, so they waved their love to him every morning, wet or fine.

All this time, Mother was kept busy with her writing, and she posted off many stories. Sometimes they would come back, but sometimes she would get a letter telling her that her story was to be printed in a magazine. Whenever this happened, Mother would wave the envelope in the air, saying, 'Hooray! Hooray! What a sensible Editor!' And then there were buns for tea.

One day, Peter was going down to the village to buy buns when he met the Station Master. Peter felt very uncomfortable after the business with the coal, but the Station Master said, 'Good morning.'

'Good morning,' replied Peter.

'Where are you off to in such a hurry?'

Peter told him about the buns.

'So, your Mother writes stories, does she?' said the Station Master. 'You should be proud to have such a clever Mother.'

'We are,' said Peter. 'But she used to play with us more before she had to be so clever.'

'Well, look in at the station whenever you feel like it,' said the Station Master. And when Peter looked surprised, he added, 'As to the matter of the coal – well – we won't ever mention that again.'

'Thank you,' said Peter, gratefully.

And the next day, after they had waved to the old gentleman, they went to the station once again. They spent a very happy two hours with the Porter, whose name was Perks. He told them many things about the railway and never seemed to tire of answering questions. The Station Master came out twice from the ticket office. He gave each of the children an orange and promised to take them up into the signal box one day when he wasn't so busy.

Several trains went through the station, and Peter noticed that the engines had numbers on them.

'I used to know a young man who collected train numbers,' said Perks. 'He put them down in a little green notebook.'

Peter thought that was a good idea, but as he didn't have a notebook Perks gave him a yellow envelope to write on. Peter wrote down two train numbers, feeling that this might be the beginning of a most interesting hobby. That evening, Mother gave him a little black notebook for his collection of numbers.

The next day, Mother stayed in bed because her head ached badly. Her hands were burning hot and her throat was sore; and she could not eat anything. Mrs Viney told her to send for the doctor.

Peter was sent to the doctor's house, and came back with Dr Forrest, a charming man who was interested in railways and rabbits and other important things. He went upstairs to see Mother, then told the children that she had influenza.

'I suppose you'll want to be head-nurse,' he said to Bobbie.

'Of course,' she said.

'Well, I'll send some medicine. Keep a good fire burning and have some strong beef tea ready for her as soon as the fever goes down. She can have grapes now, and beef-essence, and soda-water and milk. And you'd better get in a bottle of the best brandy.'

Bobbie asked him to write it all down, and he did.

But when Mother saw the list, she laughed. 'Nonsense,' she said, lying in bed with eyes as bright as beads. 'We can't afford all that. Tell Mrs Viney to boil two pounds of scrag-end of the neck for your dinners tomorrow, and I can have some of the broth.'

Later, the children talked together.

'Mother needs those things,' said Bobbie, 'and we must find a way to get them for her. Now think, everybody, just as hard as you can.'

They did think. And presently they talked. And later, when Bobbie had gone up to sit with Mother, the other two became very busy with scissors, a white sheet, a paint brush and some black paint.

Bobbie's bed had been moved into Mother's room, and several times in the night she got up to put more coal on the fire, and to give her Mother milk and soda-water.

Next morning, when the 9.15 came out of the tunnel, the old gentleman put down his newspaper ready to wave at the three children. But this morning there was only one. It was Peter.

Peter was not sitting on the fence, he was pointing at the large white sheet that was nailed to it. On it, in big black letters, were the words: LOOK OUT AT THE STATION.

A good many people did look out at the station and were disappointed, for they saw nothing unusual. It was only as the train was beginning to puff and pull itself together, ready to start again, that the old gentleman saw Phyllis running along the platform.

'Oh, I thought I'd missed you,' she gasped. 'My bootlaces kept coming undone, and I fell over them twice. Here, take it.'

She threw a warm, dampish letter into his hand as the train moved away. He leaned back in his corner, opened the letter and began to read.

Dear Mr (we do not know your name)

Mother is ill and the doctor says to give her the things at the end of the letter, but she says she can't afford it. We do not know anybody here but you, because Father is away and we do not know the address. Father will pay you, or if he has lost all his money, Peter will pay you when he is a man. We promise it on our honor. I.O.U. for all the things Mother wants.

sined PETER

Will you give the parsel to the Station Master, because we don't know which train you come down on? Say it is for Peter who was sorry about the coal, and he will know.

ROBERTA
PHYLLIS
PETER

Then came the list of things the doctor had ordered. The old gentleman read it through once and his eyebrows went up. Then he read it again and smiled.

At about six that evening, there was a knock at the back door. The three children rushed to open it, and there stood Perks, the friendly Porter, with a big hamper. He dumped it on the stone floor of the kitchen.

'Old gent,' he said. 'Asked me to fetch it up straight away.'

'Thank you very much,' said Peter. 'I'm most awfully sorry but I haven't got twopence to give you like Father does, but –'

'Stop please!' said Perks. 'Never mind about any tuppences. I only wanted to say I'm sorry your Mamma isn't well. I've brought her a bit of sweetbrier, very sweet to smell it is.' And he produced a bunch of sweetbrier from his hat, like a conjurer.

Perks left, and the children opened the hamper. Inside were all the things they had asked for, and a good many they had not – peaches,

port wine, two chickens. And a cardboard box of big red roses, and a bottle of lavender water. There was a letter, too.

Dear Roberta and Phyllis and Peter,

Here are the things you want. Your mother will want to know where they came from. Tell her they were sent by a friend who heard she was ill. When she is well again you must tell her all about it, of course. And if she says you should not have asked for the things, tell her I say that you were quite right, and that it was my great pleasure to help.

The letter was signed G.P. something – the children could not read it.

'I think we were right,' said Peter.

'Right? Of course we were right,' said Bobbie.

'All the same,' said Peter, worriedly, 'I'm not looking forward to telling Mother.'

The Engine Burglar

Two weeks after the arrival of the wonderful hamper, the old gentleman saw another banner fixed to the fence when the 9.15 passed by. It said: SHE IS NEARLY WELL, THANK YOU. He waved cheerfully from the train.

But now it was time for the children to tell Mother what they had done when she was ill. It was not easy, but they did it – and Mother was extremely angry, angrier than they had ever known her. This was horrible, but it was much worse when she began to cry. In no time at all, the children were crying, too.

Mother stopped first, and dried her eyes. 'I'm sorry I was so angry, darlings,' she said, 'because I know you didn't understand. It's quite true that we're poor, but you mustn't go telling our affairs to everyone, it's not right. And you must never, never, never ask strangers to give you things. Now always remember that, won't you?'

They all hugged her and rubbed their damp cheeks against hers and promised they would.

'I'll write a letter to your old gentleman and thank him for his kindness,' said Mother. 'You can give it to the Station Master to give him – and we won't say any more about it.'

Next day was Bobbie's birthday. In the afternoon she was told politely but firmly to stay out of the way, so she walked around the garden until it was tea-time. Then Phyllis and Peter met her at the back door. They were very clean and tidy, and Phyllis had a red bow in her hair. There was just enough time for Bobbie to make herself tidy and tie up her hair with a blue bow before they called her into the dining room.

Mother and Peter and Phyllis were standing in a row at the end of the table. The shutters were shut and there were twelve candles on the table, one for each of Bobbie's years. The table was covered with flowers, and several interesting little packages.

'Three cheers for Bobbie!' they cried, and gave them very loudly. Then they were all hugging and kissing her.

'Now,' said Mother, 'look at your presents.'

They were very nice presents. There was a green and red needle-book that Phyllis had secretly made herself. There was a little silver brooch of Mother's shaped like a buttercup, which Bobbie had known and loved for years but had never thought would be her own. There was also a pair of blue glass vases from Mrs Viney which Bobbie had seen and admired in the village shop. And there were three pretty birthday cards.

'Here's my present,' said Peter, dumping his adored steam-engine on the table. It was full of sweets. Bobbie looked surprised, because just for a moment she thought Peter was giving her his own dear little engine.

'Oh, not the engine,' he said quickly. 'Only the sweets.'

There was only the tiniest flicker of disappointment on Bobbie's face, but Peter saw it. 'I mean not all the engine,' he said. 'I'll let you have half, if you like.'

'Thank you, Peter,' said Bobbie. 'It's a splendid present.' And she thought, 'It was kind of Peter to do that. Well, the broken half shall be my half, and I'll get it mended.'

It was a delightful birthday. After tea, Mother played games with them, then nearer bedtime she read them a lovely new story.

'You won't sit up late working, will you, Mother?' said Bobbie as they kissed her good-night.

Mother said no, she wouldn't – she would just write to Father and then go to bed.

But when Bobbie crept down later to bring up her presents, Mother was not writing. Her head was on her arms and her arms were on the table.

'Mother doesn't want me to know she's unhappy,' Bobbie thought. 'And I won't know; I won't know.'

And she slipped quietly away.

Next morning, Phyllis and Peter and Mother went by train to the nearest town to do some shopping. Bobbie waited until they had gone, then she wrapped Peter's steam-engine in brown paper and took it down to the railway. There she waited patiently with it under her arm.

When the next train came in and stopped, Bobbie went across the line and stood beside the engine. She had never been so close to an engine before, and it was much larger than she had expected.

The engine driver and fireman did not see her. They were leaning out the other side, talking to the Porter.

'If you please, Mr Engineer,' Bobbie said. But the engine was blowing off steam and nobody heard her. It seemed the only way to make herself heard was to climb on to the engine, so Bobbie clambered up the high step and into the cab. She stumbled and fell on to a heap of coal.

By the time Bobbie had picked herself up, the train was moving!

Dreadful thoughts flashed through Bobbie's head. Suppose this was an express train that went on for hundreds of miles without stopping? How would she get home again? She had no money to pay for the return journey.

'I've no business here,' she thought. 'I'm an engine burglar!'

She put out a hand and touched the nearest sleeve. The man turned with a start and stared at Bobbie in surprise.

'Well, here's a bloomin' go!' said the driver – and Bobbie burst into tears.

'You're a naughty girl, that's what you are,' said the fireman.

Then they made Bobbie sit on a seat in the cab and told her to stop crying.

'I – I did call out to you, but you didn't hear me,' said Bobbie, when she had stopped crying. 'Please, don't be cross.'

'But why did you do it?' asked the fireman. 'It isn't every day a little girl tumbles into our coal bunker out of the sky, is it, Bill?'

Bobbie unwrapped the engine and showed it to them. 'I thought perhaps you might be able to mend this for me. Everyone on the railway is so kind and good, I didn't think you'd mind.'

A wink passed between the two men.

'My job is driving engines, not mending them,' said Bill. 'And how are we going to get you back to your friends and relations?'

'If you put me down at the next stop,' said Bobbie, 'and lend me the money for a ticket, I'll pay you back, honestly!'

Bill smiled. 'Don't worry, we'll see you get home safe. And about this engine – Jim, haven't you got a friend who can use a soldering iron? It's all it needs.' He turned a little brass wheel inside the real engine as he spoke.

'What is that for?' asked Bobbie.

And by the time they reached Stackpoole Junction, Bobbie learned more about the workings of a steam engine than she had ever thought there was to learn. And Jim had promised that his second cousin's wife's brother would mend Peter's engine.

Bobbie got home in time for tea.

'Where have you been?' asked the others.

'To the station, of course,' said Bobbie, but would not tell them a word about her adventures until the day when she mysteriously led them to the railway and introduced them to Bill and Jim.

Jim's second cousin's wife's brother had mended the toy engine. It was as good as new. Then, as the three children went up the hill again, Peter hugging the engine, Bobbie told them the story of how she had been an engine-burglar.

Landslide!

There were all sorts of trees beside the railway, birches and beeches and baby oaks and hazels, and amongst these were some wild cherry trees. In the spring, their blossom had shone like snow and silver. But now it was cherry time and the children had come to look for wild cherries.

They had brought their lunch in a basket, which would do to carry the cherries in if they found any. The trees grew all up and along the rocky face of the cliff out of which the mouth of the tunnel opened. Near the tunnel were some steep wooden steps, leading down to the line, and the children went along by the fence towards the little swing gate at the top.

Suddenly, Bobbie said, 'What's that?'

It was a rustling, whispering sound, quite plain above the noise of the wind and the hum of the telegraph wires.

'Look!' cried Peter. 'The trees over there!'

He was pointing across to the opposite bank where, for about twenty yards, the trees and bushes were sliding down towards the railway line.

'It – it's magic!' said Phyllis. 'I always knew the railway was magic.'

The trees moved on and on. Some stones and loose earth fell on to the railway lines below.

'It's all coming down!' said Peter. And with a great rushing sound, rock and trees and grass and bushes slipped away from the bank and crashed down in a heap on the railway line, in a huge cloud of dust.

'It's right across the down line,' said Phyllis.

'And the 11.29 down hasn't gone by yet,' said Peter. 'We must let them know at the station or there'll be a terrible accident.'

'Let's run,' said Bobbie.

'Wait,' said Peter. 'There isn't time. It's ten miles away and it's past eleven now.'

'Couldn't we climb up the telegraph post and do something to the wires,' said Phyllis. 'They do it in war, I've heard about it.'

'They only cut the lines, silly,' said Peter. 'And that won't do any good. If we had anything red, we could go down on the line and wave it.'

They climbed down the wooden steps, pale and worried.

Bobbie turned at the bottom of the steps. 'Our flannel petticoats!' she said. 'They're red. Let's take them off.'

So Phyllis and Bobbie took off their petticoats and the three children ran along the line to the corner where, once round it, the heap of stones and trees could not be seen. Peter took the largest petticoat.

'You're not going to . . . tear them, are you?' said Phyllis.

'Yes, tear them into little bits, if you like,' said Bobbie. 'Don't you see, Phil, if we can't stop the train there'll be a terrible accident.'

They tore the petticoats into six strips, then tied them to sticks to make them into flags. Two were pushed into heaps of little stones along the line, then Bobbie and Phyllis each took one, and Peter took the other two.

They seemed to wait for hours, but then came the distant rumble and hum of the lines, and a puff of white steam far away.

'Stand firm, and wave like mad!' said Peter. 'Don't stand on the line, Bobbie!'

The train rattled towards them. The two flags on the line swayed and fell over, and Bobbie picked one of them up.

'It's no good!' she cried. 'They won't see us!'

'Keep off the line, you silly cuckoo!' said Peter.

But Bobbie waved her two flags right over the line. The front of the engine looked black and enormous.

'Stop! Stop!' she shouted, but the noise of the train drowned her voice.

Suddenly, it began to slow down . . . slower . . . slower . . . until it stopped – not twenty yards from Bobbie. She saw the big black engine stop, but somehow she could not stop waving her flags. And when the driver and the fireman got off the engine, and Peter and Phyllis went to meet them and explain, Bobbie still waved the flags. But when they turned to see where she was, Bobbie was lying on the line.

'She fainted!' said the driver, hurrying towards her, the others following.

The driver picked Bobbie up and carried her back to the train, where he laid her on the cushions of a first-class carriage.

'I'll just have a look at this landslide,' said the driver, 'then I'll run you back to the station.'

Bobbie lay white and quiet as the train went back to the station, but opened her eyes just before they got there.

'Well done!' said everyone at the station, when they were told what the children had done. Suddenly, Bobbie, Peter and Phyllis were heroes. Phyllis and Peter enjoyed this very much, but Bobbie just wanted to go home. As they did so, everyone on the platform gave a loud cheer.

It was only when they were halfway home that Bobbie remembered something. 'We never got any cherries, after all,' she said.

One morning, a few weeks later, a letter arrived. It was addressed to Peter and Bobbie and Phyllis. It said:

Dear Sir, and Ladies,

We would like to make a small presentation to you, to thank you for your prompt and courageous action which saved the train from a terrible accident. The presentation will take place at three o'clock on the 30th of the month, if this is convenient to you.

Yours faithfully,
Jabez Inglewood
Secretary, Great Northern and Southern Railway Company

There had never been a prouder moment in the lives of the three children. They rushed to Mother with the letter, who was also very proud.

'A presentation means presents,' said Peter. 'Whatever will it be?'

'It might be anything,' said Phyllis. 'I've always wanted a baby elephant – but they wouldn't know that.'

When at last the day came, the three children went down to the station at the proper time, dressed in their smartest and prettiest clothes. And everything that happened seemed like a dream. The Station Master came to meet them, and led them into the waiting room where a carpet had been put down and flowers put on the mantelpiece and window-ledges. There were quite a number of people there, besides the Porter and everybody who belonged at the station – ladies in smart dresses, and gentlemen in high hats and frock coats. They recognised several people who had been on the train on red-flannel-petticoat day.

But best of all, their own old gentleman was there, and he came to shake hands with them. Then everyone sat down, and the District Superintendent began to make a speech. He said all sorts of nice things about the children's bravery, then he sat down and everyone clapped.

Next, the old gentleman got up and said nice things, too. Then he called the children one by one and gave them each a beautiful gold watch and chain. Inside each watch was engraved the name of the new owner, and there was a blue leather case to keep it in.

'You must make a speech and thank everybody,' whispered the Station Master in Peter's ear.

'Oh dear,' said Peter, as he was pushed forward. 'Er – ladies and gentlemen, it's very good of you, and we shall treasure the watches all our lives – but what we did wasn't anything really – I mean, it was awfully exciting but – er – and what I mean to say is – thank you all very, very much.'

The people clapped and everybody wanted to shake hands with them. But as soon as it was polite to do so, the children ran back up the hill to Three Chimneys with their watches in their hands.

'Why didn't you go with them?' he said.

'Somebody had to stay with you,' Bobbie said. 'I must put out the candle now because there may not be enough of the other one left to get you out.'

'You think of everything,' he said.

She blew it out and they sat in the black-velvety darkness.

'Aren't you afraid of the dark, Bobbie?' he said.

'Not – not very, that is –'

'Let's hold hands,' said the boy.

The darkness was more bearable now that her small hand was held in his big rough one. She tried to talk, to keep his mind off his broken leg, but it was difficult. It was also cold in the tunnel.

After a while, they both fell asleep in the darkness.

And that was how Peter and Phyllis found them when they came back with some men from a nearby farm. The men had made a makeshift stretcher for carrying Jim.

'Where does he live?' one of them asked.

'In Northumberland,' answered Bobbie.

'I'm at school at Maidenbridge,' said Jim. 'I suppose I've got to get back there somehow.'

'The doctor ought to have a look at you first,' said the man.

'Bring him to our house,' said Bobbie. 'It's only a little way, and I'm sure Mother would say we ought to.'

So Jim was lifted up on the stretcher and carried out of the dark tunnel and into the sunshine once more. He was taken to Three Chimneys where Mother was surprised to see the little procession coming towards the house. But she immediately made up a bed for Jim and then called the doctor.

'I hate to give you all this trouble,' said Jim.

'Don't you worry,' said Mother. 'It's you that have the trouble, you poor dear.'

She did not get back to her writing that day, except to write to Jim's grandfather who, Jim said, lived not too far away; and to send a message to the school.

The doctor came to look at Jim's leg and said that it was a clean break and would mend without any trouble.

'He can rest here whilst it's mending,' said Mother.

And this pleased the children greatly.

Jim's Grandfather

It was soon after breakfast the next day that a knock came at the door. The children were hard at work cleaning the brass candlesticks in honour of Jim's visit.

'That'll be the doctor again,' said Mother. 'I'll go. Shut the kitchen door.'

But it wasn't the doctor. They knew by the voice and the sound of the boots that went upstairs. But whose voice was it? They were sure they had heard it before somewhere.

Shortly after, they heard Mother's voice from the top of the stairs. 'Bobbie!'

They opened the kitchen door and saw Mother leaning over the stair railing.

'Jim's grandfather has come,' she said. 'Wash your hands and faces, he wants to see you.'

They were busy doing this when they heard the boots and the voices come downstairs again and go into the dining room. The children followed as quickly as they could.

Mother was sitting in the window seat, but in the leather-covered armchair sat – THEIR OWN OLD GENTLEMAN!

'It's you!' cried Bobbie. Then remembered her manners and said, 'How do you do?' very nicely.

'How splendid,' said Peter.

'I'm awfully glad it is you,' said Phyllis. 'When you think of all the old gentlemen there are in the world, it might have been almost anyone.'

The old gentleman smiled.

'But you're not going to take Jim away, are you?' said Peter.

'Not at present,' said the old gentleman. 'Your Mother has kindly agreed to let him stay here, and she's even willing to nurse him.'

'But what about her writing?' said Peter, before anyone could stop him. 'There won't be anything to eat if she doesn't write.'

The old gentleman looked at Mother. 'May I tell them our little arrangement?' He turned to the children. 'Your Mother has agreed to give up writing for a while and become Matron of my hospital.'

'Oh!' said Phyllis. 'Shall we have to go away from Three Chimneys and the railway and everything?'

'No, no, darling,' said Mother, hurriedly.

'The hospital is called Three Chimneys Hospital,' said the old gentleman, 'and my unlucky Jim is the only patient. But there will be a housekeeper and a cook to help her until Jim is well.'

'And then will Mother go on writing again?' asked Peter.

'We shall see,' said the old gentleman, with a quick glance at Bobbie. 'Perhaps something nice will happen and she won't have to.'

"I love my writing,' said Mother, very quickly.

'I know,' he said, 'and don't be afraid that I'm going to interfere. But wonderful things do happen, don't they? And we live our lives hoping for them.' He looked at the children. 'Take care of your Mother, my dears. She's a woman in a million. Now, will Bobbie come with me to the gate?'

When the two of them were outside, at the gate, the old gentleman said, 'You're a good child, and I got your letter, but it wasn't needed. When I read about your Father's case in the papers at the time, I had my doubts. Ever since I've known who you were, I've been trying to find out things. I haven't done very much yet, but I have hopes, my dear.'

'Oh!' said Bobbie, choking a little.

'Yes, great hopes. But keep your secret a little longer. It wouldn't do to upset your Mother with false hopes.'

'You don't think Father did it, do you?' said Bobbie. 'Oh, say you don't think he did!'

'My dear,' said the old gentleman, 'I'm perfectly certain he didn't.'

The End

Life at Three chimneys was never quite the same again after the old gentleman came to see his grandson. Although the children knew his name now, they never called him by it. To them, he was always the old gentleman.

As Jim got better, the children sat and listened to his tales about school life and the other boys; and he taught Peter how to play chess and draughts. And now that Mother wasn't writing every day, she was able to teach the children their lessons. Altogether, there seemed little time for the railway any more and each of the children had uneasy feelings about this which, one day, Phyllis put into words.

'I wonder if the railway misses us,' she said. 'We never go to see it now.'

'It seems ungrateful,' said Bobbie. 'We loved it so when we hadn't anyone to play with. And we don't wave to the Green Dragon and send our love to Father any more. That's what I don't like.'

'Let's begin again,' said Phyllis.

And they did.

It was September now and the turf on the slope was dry and crisp as they ran down to the railway the next morning.

"Hurry up!' said Peter. 'Or we shall miss the 9.15.'

'I can't hurry any more,' said Phyllis. 'Oh, my bootlace has come undone again!'

'When you get married,' said Peter, laughing, 'your bootlace will come undone as you walk up the church aisle, and your man will fall over it on to his nose! Oh, look, the signal's down. We must run.'

They ran. And once more they were able to wave their handkerchiefs at the 9.15.

'Take our love to Father!' they shouted.

The old gentleman waved from his carriage window, and there was nothing odd in that for he had always waved. But now handkerchiefs fluttered, newspapers signalled and hands waved wildly from every window of the train! It swept by with a rustle and a roar and the children were left looking at one another.

'Well!' said Peter

'Well!' said Bobbie.

'WELL!' said Phyllis.

'Whatever does it mean?' said Peter.

'Perhaps the old gentleman told the people to look out for us and wave because he knew we'd like it,' said Bobbie. But she had a strange feeling somewhere deep inside her, as though something was about to happen.

And later, when they were having their lessons with Mother, Bobbie found it hard to concentrate. She got most of her sums wrong, then dropped her slate so that it cracked across the middle.

'What is it?' asked Mother. 'Do you feel ill?'

'I don't know,' said Bobbie. 'I feel as if I want to be by myself. Perhaps I'll be better in the garden.'

But she couldn't stay in the garden. The hollyhocks and asters and late roses all seemed to be waiting for something to happen. It was one of those still, shiny autumn days when everything does seem to be waiting.

'I'll go down to the station and talk to Perks,' Bobbie thought.

On the way, she passed the old lady from the Post Office, who gave her a kiss and a hug, to Bobbie's surprise. 'God bless you, love,' the woman said. 'Run along, do.'

Several other people waved their newspapers and smiled at Bobbie as she went by, and at the station the Station Master shook her hand warmly and said, 'The 11.54's a bit late, Miss,' then went quickly into his room.

Perks was nowhere to be seen and Bobbie shared the empty platform with the station cat. 'How very kind everybody is today,' she said, stroking the animal.

Perks appeared when the 11.54 was signalled. He, like everybody else that morning, had a newspaper in his hand.

'Hallo,' he said. 'Here you are then. God bless you, my dear. I saw it in the paper, and I've never been so glad about anything in all my days!' And with that, he kissed her first on one cheek and then on the other. 'You don't mind me doing that, do you? On a day like this –'

'No I don't mind,' said Bobbie. 'But on a day like what? And what did you see in the paper?'

But already the 11.54 was steaming into the station and Perks was looking in all the windows.

Only three people got off the train. The first was a woman with three baskety-boxes full of live chickens. The second was Miss Peckitt, the grocer's wife's cousin, with a tin box and three brown-paper parcels.

And the third . . .

'Oh! My Daddy, my Daddy!' That scream went like a knife into the heart of everyone in the train. People put their heads out of the windows to see a tall pale man with lips set in a thin close line, and a little girl clinging to him with arms and legs, while his arms went tightly round her.

'I knew something wonderful was going to happen,' said Bobbie, as they went up the road, 'but I didn't think it was going to be this. Oh,

my Daddy, my Daddy!'

'Didn't Mother get my letter?' Father asked.

'There weren't any letters this morning. Oh, Daddy, it really is you, isn't it?'

He clasped her hand tightly and assured her it was. Then he said, 'You must go in by yourself and tell Mother quite quietly that it's all right. They've caught the man who did it. Everyone knows now that it wasn't your Daddy.'

'I always knew it wasn't,' said Bobbie. 'Me and Mother and our old gentleman.'

'Yes,' he said. 'It's all thanks to him. Mother wrote and told me you had found out. And she told me what a help you've been to her. My own little girl!' They stopped a minute then.

. . . And now they are crossing the field. Bobbie goes into the house, trying to find the right words to 'tell Mother quite quietly' that the sorrow and the struggle and the parting are over, and that Father has come home.

Father is walking in the garden, waiting – waiting. He is looking at the flowers, but his eyes keep turning towards the house. And presently he leaves the garden and goes and stands outside the back door. Across the yard, swallows are circling, signalling the end of the summer.

Now the door opens. Bobbie's voice calls:

'Come in, Daddy. Come in!'

He goes in and the door shuts behind him.

I think it will be best for us to go quickly and quietly away. But we may take just one last look, over our shoulders, at the white house where neither we nor anyone else is wanted now.